P9-CQP-418

THE GOLDEN BOOK OF
SNAKES
AND OTHER REPTILES

By Steven Lindblom / Illustrated by James Spence

John L. Behler, Curator, Department of Herpetology,
New York Zoological Society, Consultant

A GOLDEN BOOK • NEW YORK

Western Publishing Company, Inc., Racine, Wisconsin 53404

© 1990 Steven Lindblom. Illustrations © 1990 James Spence. All rights reserved. Printed in the U.S.A.
No part of this book may be reproduced or copied in any form without written permission from the publisher.
All trademarks are the property of Western Publishing Company, Inc. Library of Congress Catalog Card
Number: 89-80558 ISBN: 0-307-15852-7/ISBN: 0-307-65852-X (lib. bdg.)   A B C D E F G H I J K L M

WHAT IS A REPTILE?

Reptiles have existed for over 300 million years. That is much longer than man has been around—only about two million years. The earliest reptiles were among the first animals to emerge from the sea and live on land, and scientists believe that most of today's animal life evolved from them.

Reptiles are air-breathing animals. They have lungs like we do, not gills like fish. Even reptiles that live underwater must regularly come up for air.

Reptiles are also cold-blooded animals whose body temperature varies according to that of the air or water around them. They rely on the sun to warm them and give them energy. That is why reptiles are most common in the warmer parts of Earth and cannot live where the weather is very cold year-round.

On the other hand, man and other mammals are warm-blooded. No matter how hot or cold the weather becomes, a mammal's body temperature always stays the same. Mammals use energy from food to keep their bodies warm.

Dimetrodon

Being cold-blooded has advantages and disadvantages. When a reptile gets cold, it gets sluggish and moves slowly. It can neither hunt well nor run from other animals until it warms up. But since cold-blooded animals don't need food energy to keep warm, they can survive by eating much less food than a mammal needs.

Reptiles are outnumbered today by warm-blooded mammals, but that wasn't always the case. From the time of those first reptiles until the end of the age of dinosaurs 250 million years later, reptiles ruled Earth. Reptiles flew in the skies and swam in the seas. But while most of these wonderful reptiles disappeared, others survived and are with us today.

Scientists now divide reptiles into four groups called orders. Three of these orders are: snakes and lizards; crocodilians; and turtles. The fourth order includes just one species, the tuatara, a lizardlike creature found only on about 30 small islands off the coasts of New Zealand. Turtles and crocodilians have changed so little since the age of dinosaurs that seeing them today gives us a rare glimpse of the past.

phytosaur

alligator snapper

SNAKES

Snakes are perhaps the best-known reptiles, and they are very easy to identify. They have no legs, eyelids, or ear openings. They range in size from a few inches to over 30 feet long, but the longest North American snakes are rarely more than 8 feet long.

Lying hidden in the leaves or slipping silently through the grass, snakes have a way of taking us by surprise. Many people are afraid of snakes, but no snake found in North America will go out of its way to attack a human. If a snake did try, a person could easily outrun it. Most people who get bitten by snakes either step on them by accident or handle them carelessly. Bites from nonvenomous snakes can hurt but are no more dangerous than small cuts or scratches. Venomous snakes, of course, are very dangerous, but they are rare in most parts of the United States.

When seen up close, snakes can be recognized for the beautiful, graceful creatures they are. Most snakes live useful lives, eating rats, mice, and other pests. The snakes we are most likely to meet are peaceful, harmless creatures, well worth getting to know better.

grass snake

8

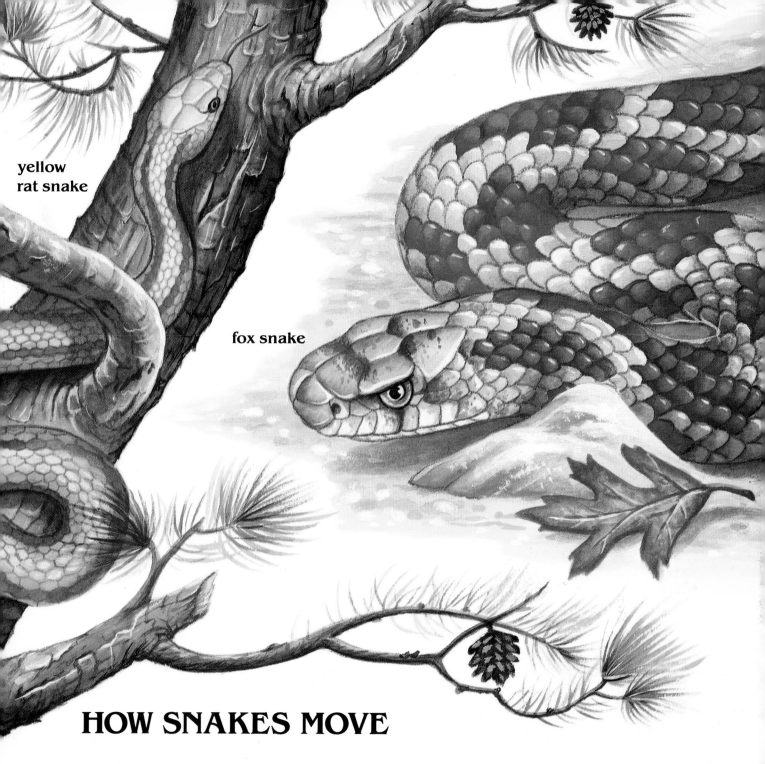

yellow
rat snake

fox snake

HOW SNAKES MOVE

Snakes have several ways of moving. Usually they move forward by flexing their bodies against rocks, plants, and other objects to propel themselves. If there is nothing around to push against, they can still crawl, using their wide belly scales called scutes. The scutes are attached to muscles that let snakes move the scutes in and out to get a grip on the ground and pull themselves along.

Most snakes are also good swimmers. They slither through the water as gracefully as they crawl across the ground. Many of them are good climbers as well.

9

RINGNECK SNAKES AND SHEDDING

A tiny ringneck snake twists and squirms as it sheds its old skin. First the snake rubs against a rock until the old skin across its snout splits open. Then the snake wiggles out of the old skin. Underneath is bright new smooth skin.

As the time to shed approaches, the snake's old skin becomes dull. The skin over the eyes also becomes clouded, until the ringneck snake is almost blind. The snake must feel better when the shedding is over.

All snakes wear out their skins through crawling around, and they shed several times a year. Young, fast-growing snakes shed even more often than older snakes.

ROUGH GREEN SNAKES

A rough green snake crawls along a tree branch, almost invisible among the green leaves. The rough green snake gets its name from its rough scales, which help it to climb trees. This slender, graceful snake lives in trees and bushes, slithering through the leaves and branches to feed on spiders, crickets, and caterpillars.

Like most snakes, the rough green snake is colored to blend in with its surroundings. This special coloring helps snakes to sneak up on their prey and to hide from their enemies.

Another green snake, the smooth green snake, has smooth scales. Although it is able to climb, this snake lives on the ground and is often called a grass snake.

11

WATER SNAKES

A banded water snake suns itself by a bush while a fat common water snake glides through the water of a quiet swamp in search of a meal. Snakes, like most reptiles, are skillful hunters. They rarely pursue their prey, and prefer to sneak up on their victims and take them by surprise.

Water snakes are found mostly in the eastern half of the United States. They are good swimmers and spend their lives in or near water. Water snakes look dangerous and are often mistaken for venomous water moccasins. This resemblance causes people to leave water snakes alone, which is just as well, since their bite, while not venomous, can be painful.

water snake

Northern water snake

MILK SNAKES

A milk snake waits quietly for its meal, which is hidden beneath the floor of a barn. Mice often live in barns and eat the grain that spills down from cows' feed troughs. Milk snakes feed on the mice. Old folktales have it that milk snakes suck milk from cows, but the mice are what really keep the snakes near barns. If surprised, milk snakes may coil themselves as if to strike and shake their tails like rattlesnakes. But they are nonvenomous and harmless.

BABY SNAKES

Its 12 new eggs left hidden beside a rock, a mother corn snake glides off to look for something to eat. While some mother snakes guard their eggs, they will not feed or care for the baby snakes once they hatch. Each baby snake will cut its way out of its egg using a tiny sharp spur on its nose called an egg tooth. The baby corn snakes will become the large handsome snakes often found in abandoned buildings hunting for mice and rats.

In the woods nearby, a DeKay's, or brown, snake may be giving birth to a litter of 18 baby snakes, each no bigger than a matchstick. Some snakes carry their eggs inside their bodies until they hatch, so their young are born alive. When fully grown, these gentle and harmless DeKay's snakes will be only one foot long.

INDIGO SNAKES

Indigo snakes are among the longest snakes in North America. They can grow to be eight feet long. Farmers like these beautiful dark-blue snakes because they eat rats and other creatures that could otherwise destroy crops.

Indigo snakes are quick to get used to people. Once they do, they even seem to like being handled. This has made them a favorite of circus snake charmers.

GARTER SNAKES

If caught sunning themselves on an old stone wall, garter snakes would be quick to hide among the rocks. Garter snakes are among the most common snakes in America and are easily recognized by their bright stripes.

In cold weather snakes must warm themselves in the sun before they can move quickly. Similarly, to cool off, snakes must get out of the sun, so they spend their days shuttling between sun and shade to keep comfortable.

When winter comes, garter snakes, like all reptiles living in colder climates, must find warm shelter. They crawl into caves to sleep away the winter, sometimes tangled together with other garter snakes.

COACHWHIP SNAKES

A long, slender coachwhip snake glides through the grass, flicking its forked tongue in and out. A snake's tongue is harmless; it cannot sting or hurt. Snakes use their tongues to both feel and "smell-taste" things. Their tongues pick up tiny bits of scent and bring them to the snakes' mouths to taste. When snakes flick their tongues at something, the snakes are just taking a little taste and trying to figure out what is around them.

Coachwhip snakes and their close relatives, racers, are found all over the United States. As their names suggest, they are among the fastest-moving snakes, reaching top speeds of seven miles an hour.

RAT SNAKES

A rat snake has just stolen three eggs from a bird's nest and swallowed them whole. They make three uncomfortable-looking lumps in the snake's throat. But the rat snake doesn't mind. Like all snakes, rat snakes can open their jaws very wide and their skin can stretch to allow the snakes to swallow things much wider than themselves.

All snakes are carnivorous, which means that they feed on live insects, fish, frogs, mice, and other small animals rather than on plants. Unlike mammals, which need many meals to maintain high energy levels, snakes can go for a long time without eating. In fact, some snakes in captivity have been known to go for as long as two years without a meal!

HOGNOSE SNAKES

A hognose snake pokes the ground with its hard turned-up nose, looking for a toad to eat. If someone disturbs them, hognose snakes will flatten their heads, make a loud hissing noise, and strike. But instead of biting, they will merely hit with their noses! If that doesn't scare the person away, hognose snakes will roll onto their backs and play dead. They will continue to hang limp even when picked up. If put back down right-side up, hognose snakes will give themselves away by turning over on their backs again.

VENOMOUS SNAKES

Relatively few of the snakes in America are venomous. Except for coral snakes, which are slender and strikingly colored, venomous snakes are recognized by their fat bodies, short tails, large triangular heads, and blotched or crossbanded patterns.

Rattlesnakes, copperheads, and cottonmouths all belong to a group of snakes called pit vipers. On each side of their heads, between the eyes and the nostrils, pit vipers have little hollows or pits that can sense heat. Pit vipers use their pits like an extra set of eyes that can see in the dark. The pits help to detect a mouse—or a human hand— a foot away.

Venomous snakes have glands behind their eyes that produce venom. These snakes have hollow fangs near the front of the upper jaw, through which the venom passes when they bite.

Snake venom can be deadly to humans. However, its real purpose is to subdue snakes' prey, not to harm people. Venomous snakes are usually no more likely to attack people than are nonvenomous ones.

banded rock rattlesnake

cottonmouth

COTTONMOUTHS AND COPPERHEADS

Cottonmouths, or "water moccasins," live in swamps in the deep South, where they feed on frogs and fish. For such a fat snake the cottonmouth is a surprisingly good climber. It can often be found sunning itself on a low tree branch. It also crawls through shrubbery looking for birds' nests.

Copperheads prefer woodland. Copperheads are easy to identify because of the hourglass-shaped markings on their backs. Unlike aggressive cottonmouths, copperheads will rarely bite unless cornered. They will often face an enemy as if about to strike, while they are really slithering backward to escape.

copperhead

RATTLESNAKES

Rattlesnakes, like eastern diamondbacks, are easy to identify because of the rattles on their tails. Some people think we can tell the age of a rattler if we count its rattles, but this is not true. A rattlesnake grows another rattle every time it sheds its skin. This usually happens about three times a year. But rattles are made of hard, brittle skin that can break off. An older snake will usually have lost a few of its rattles; therefore it is rare to find a rattlesnake with more than a dozen rattles, even if it is 25 years old.

Diamondbacks are among the most deadly snakes found anywhere in the world. They are North America's largest venomous snakes and can grow to be eight feet long.

SIDEWINDERS

While hiding half-buried in the desert sand a sidewinder is almost invisible. Sidewinders are small rattlers that can be identified by the special scales over their eyes. These scales may help protect sidewinders' eyes from sand.

The sidewinder gets its name from the way it moves. On very fine, slippery sand, which makes crawling difficult, the sidewinder moves in a very complicated way. It almost looks like a rolling spiral.

CORAL SNAKES

Coral snakes are related to cobras and have the most deadly venom of any snake in North America. Luckily they also have very short fangs and are not easily provoked; therefore they rarely harm people. Coral snakes spend most of their lives burrowing beneath the ground and eating lizards and small snakes. They aren't often seen above the ground during the day.

Two harmless nonvenomous snakes, the scarlet kingsnake and the rarely seen scarlet snake, are often mistaken for the venomous coral snake.

New Guinea tree python

SNAKES OF OTHER LANDS

Some of the best-known and largest snakes, such as pythons, are not found in North America. The reticulated python of Southeast Asia is the longest snake in the world and can grow to a length of more than 30 feet. Half a world away in South America lives the anaconda. It may not be as long as the python, but it is fatter and heavier. An anaconda was once caught that weighed 600 pounds!

Another South American snake, the boa constrictor, is one of the best-known snakes in the world. It gets its name and reputation from the way it kills its prey. It coils around and squeezes its victim until the victim is smothered. Many other snakes of all sizes, including the milk snake, are also constrictors.

The jungles of India are home to many strange and wondrous snakes. Flying snakes live in the trees. They can leap from branch to branch, and by flattening their bodies they can glide from tree to tree like flying squirrels.

Below, on the jungle floor, a king cobra watches, hoping a flying snake will land near it. The king cobra feeds almost entirely on other snakes. The biggest venomous snake of all, it can grow to be over 18 feet long. With the lower part of its body still coiled on the ground, it can lift its head more than five feet high into the air.

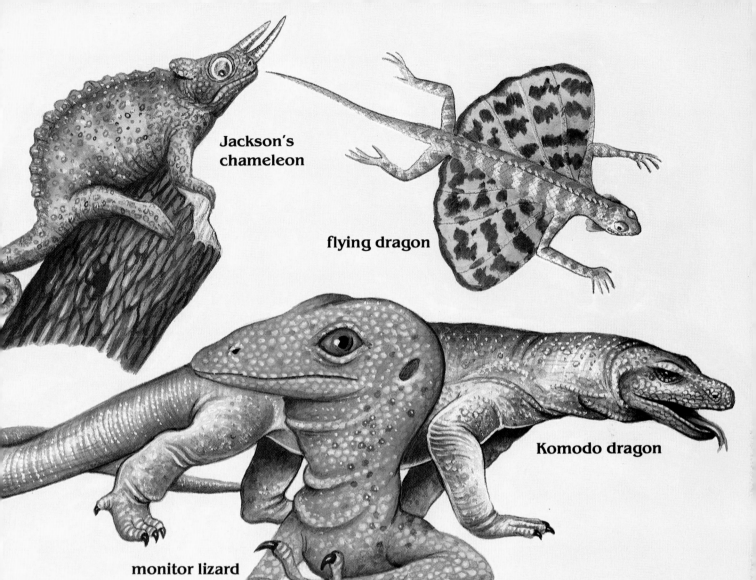

Jackson's chameleon

flying dragon

Komodo dragon

monitor lizard

LIZARDS

There are almost 3,800 different kinds of lizards, and most of them have many things in common. Most lizards have four legs, scaly skin, eyelids, and an ear opening on each side of their heads. They range in size, however, from the tiny wormlike skink to the ten-foot-long Komodo dragon of Indonesia. The biggest lizard in the United States, the Gila monster, is two feet long.

There are lizards that can swim and lizards that can dive deep beneath the ocean. Others can glide from tree to tree, walk on walls, burrow in the ground, or run on their hind legs. Like most reptiles, lizards are more common in hot climates, and the desert is home to a great many of them.

AMERICAN CHAMELEONS

The American chameleon is not a chameleon at all but a lizard called a green anole. It is called a chameleon because, like the true chameleon of Africa, an anole can change its color—from bright green to brown. When it is scared, it can turn brown in seconds to blend in with its background.

The green anole is a graceful, slender lizard with five toes on each foot. The toes have pads with ridges that allow the anole to walk up the sides of things. It is often found walking up the walls of houses in the South.

The gecko is another sure-footed wall-climbing lizard found all over the South and Southwest. Anoles and geckos are among the few reptiles that many people don't mind finding in their homes, since these little lizards eat flies, mosquitoes, and other insects.

knight anole

fan-footed gecko

28

CHUCKWALLAS AND COLLARED LIZARDS

A chuckwalla suns itself in the desert while a collared lizard dashes by. The collared lizard is a foot-long colorful lizard that can run on its hind legs when it is being chased.

The chuckwalla is the second largest lizard in the country, and one of the few that eats plants. It feeds on a variety of desert plants, including cactus fruits. If a chuckwalla is chased, it will squeeze itself in between rocks. Then it will take a deep breath to inflate its body so that it can't be pulled out!

collared lizard

chuckwalla

29

GILA MONSTERS

A Gila monster from the southwestern United States crawls along on stubby legs looking for something to eat. Gila monsters move slowly and rarely lift their bodies far off the ground. However, Gila monsters can strike suddenly if provoked. Their bite is venomous and their grip is firm. The colorful Gila monster is the biggest lizard found in the United States and the only venomous one. The closely related Mexican beaded lizard is the world's only other venomous lizard.

SKINKS

A young blue-tailed skink pokes around a rotten log looking for insects to eat. As skinks get older the bright yellow lines on their bodies fade away, and they change from shiny black to dull brown.

Members of the skink family are found all over the country. Unlike other sun-loving lizards, skinks prefer deep, shady woods, where they scurry about in search of insects and spiders. Skinks are small, less than a foot long.

People often mistake smaller skinks for salamanders. Salamanders, however, are not reptiles. They belong to another class of animals called amphibians, which also includes frogs and toads. Skinks' scaly skin and clawed feet identify them as reptiles.

HORNED LIZARDS

A horned lizard waits for an insect to come within reach of its tongue. Like snakes, lizards use their tongues to sense their surroundings. But many lizards' tongues do other jobs as well. Geckos use their tongues like windshield wipers to clean their lidless eyes. Horned lizards' tongues are long and sticky and good for catching insects.

Occasionally called "horny toad" in error, the little horned lizard is a common sight throughout the West. If frightened, a horned lizard may flatten itself against the ground as if trying to disappear. Or it may puff itself up to try to look bigger and tougher. When threatened, a horned lizard can even shoot a thin stream of blood from the corner of its eyes!

LEGLESS LIZARDS

Glass lizards are perhaps the strangest lizards of all. Even though they are legless like snakes, scientists classify them as lizards because they have lizards' heads and ear openings, and lizards' scales on their bellies. The glass lizard, like a number of other lizards, can lose its tail if handled roughly, or when trying to escape from a predator's grip. It will grow another one, but the new tail will be shorter than the old one.

Another legless reptile, the worm lizard, relies on its sense of touch as it burrows through the ground in search of ants and termites.

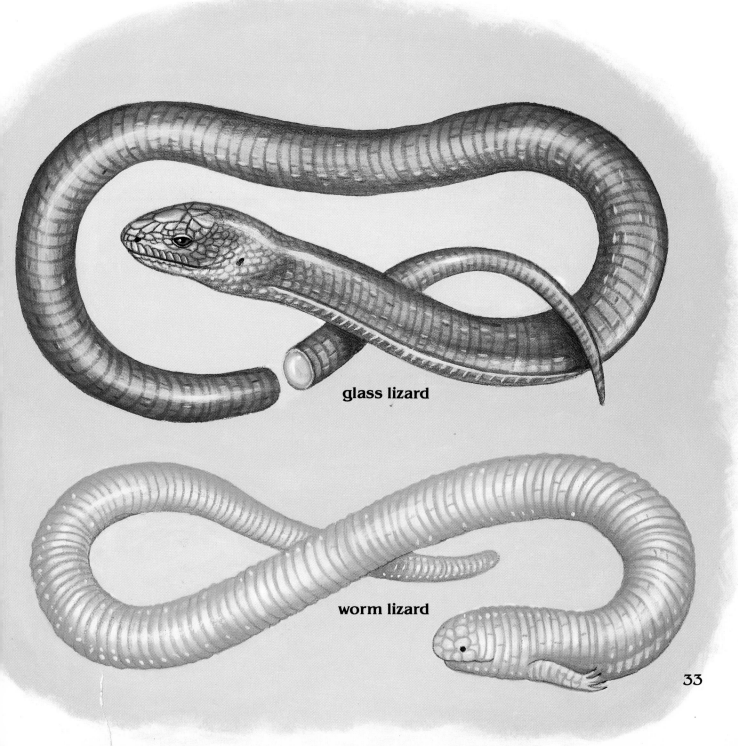

glass lizard

worm lizard

CROCODILIANS

Alligators and crocodiles are both crocodilians. They are North America's largest living reptiles and are found only in the deep South. Alligators prefer freshwater areas, where they sun themselves and feed on turtles, muskrats, raccoons, and other water creatures. Crocodiles can be found in saltwater marshes and sometimes even in the ocean.

Alligators and crocodiles differ both in their snouts and in their colors. Alligators have wide, rounded snouts, while crocodiles have long, pointed snouts with a large tooth that sticks out on each side of the lower jaw when their mouths are shut. Adult alligators are black, while crocodiles are a lighter grayish green.

Crocodilians are among the few reptiles that can make a loud noise—it sounds like a deep-throated roar.

alligator

crocodile

Crocodilians are good swimmers. They use their tails and legs to paddle along. When they are in a hurry, they can tuck their legs up against their bodies and use their powerful tails to propel them through the water.

On land, both alligators and crocodiles can stand up on their strong legs. They can lift their bodies completely off the ground and move with surprising speed.

Crocodilians are unusual reptiles because they care for and protect their young.

Their fierce looks have given all crocodilians worse reputations than they deserve. North American alligators and crocodiles rarely attack people and typically back away from them. However, nesting animals or those protecting hatchlings may be quite aggressive.

sea turtle

tortoise

snapping turtle

TURTLES

Turtles first walked on Earth 200 million years ago, long before mammals, lizards, snakes, or even dinosaurs. Their descendants are still around today.

Turtles are four-legged reptiles with short tails and strong beaklike jaws. They have no teeth. The turtle's most distinctive feature is its shell, which is made of bone and usually covered with large platelike scales. The turtle's shell is designed to protect it from predators. While a turtle can never come out of its shell, it may withdraw into it if threatened.

Turtle shells are not all the same. Slow-moving land turtles and tortoises have high-domed sturdy shells that provide the best protection against predators. Water turtles have flatter, more streamlined shells better suited for swimming. Snappers often have shells that are too small in proportion to their bodies, so they cannot draw their heads and necks all the way inside. They must depend on their fierce snapping jaws for protection.

Turtles are very long-lived. Box turtles have lived as long as 50 years in captivity. Other turtles are on record as having lived more than 100 years in captivity.

PAINTED TURTLES

A row of painted turtles that are enjoying the sun will tumble off their log and into the water if anyone gets too close. These colorful turtles are found in lakes and lily ponds over much of North America. Small aquatic turtles like painted turtles are fairly well known because they are often found sunning themselves.

The pond slider of our South, a close relative of the painted turtle, is also very fond of basking in the sun. Dozens may be seen stacked one upon another on a favorite log. These are the ``dime store'' turtles that were once sold by the millions.

BOX TURTLES

Box turtles live on land and are among the few turtles that can completely enclose themselves in their shells. If startled, they will pull their heads, legs, and tails into their shells and shut the hinged bottom shell, or plastron. In the fall when berries ripen, box turtles often eat so many that they get too fat to close their shells!

When cold weather begins, box turtles dig into loose soil, burrow deep into piles of leaves, or crawl into old stump holes to hibernate until warm weather comes again.

SNAPPERS

Snappers are big, aggressive turtles. They live in quiet streams, lakes, and ponds and eat aquatic plants and insects, crayfish, frogs, and birds. Despite their reputation, snappers are afraid of people. Usually snappers only bite people when they are lifted out of water or teased.

An alligator snapper lies patiently on the muddy bottom of a Louisiana swamp and fishes for its supper, using its pink tongue for bait. Pretty soon a fish will mistake the wiggling tongue for a worm, and the snapper will have its meal. Alligator snappers are among the biggest of the world's freshwater turtles and can weigh 150 pounds.

musk turtle

MUSK TURTLES
AND MUD TURTLES

Musk turtles look like little snappers. They are a muddy brown color, and their shells—like snappers' shells—are usually covered with algae. But bright yellow or white lines on each side of their heads add spots of color that distinguish them from snappers.

Musk turtles rarely leave the water. They sun themselves on water plants or in muddy shallows but spend much of the day resting on the bottom or buried in its mud. They get their name—and a few nicknames like stinking turtle and stinkpot—from the musky odor they give off when handled.

Mud turtles look very much like musk turtles but they have a double-hinged lower shell like a box turtle. Both musk and mud turtles are usually less then five inches long and are fond of aquatic insects and snails.

SEA TURTLES

Sea turtles are very different from freshwater turtles, because they are built for lives at sea. Instead of legs with webbed feet and claws, good for both swimming and climbing, sea turtles have powerful flippers that look almost like wings. They spend their entire lives at sea and only crawl clumsily onto land when it is time to lay their eggs.

Sea turtles are also larger than freshwater turtles. The leatherback sea turtle may reach eight feet in length and nearly a ton in weight. It is the biggest turtle of all and has changed very little since the age of dinosaurs. Its streamlined shell is made of thick leathery skin with bony plates underneath.

leatherback
sea turtle

REPTILES AS PETS

While some reptiles make good pets, others do poorly in captivity. Often they will not eat. Many reptiles, especially snakes, eat only live food in the wild and refuse to eat anything else in captivity. They must be fed live food—usually mice or frogs—which may be hard to find.

Turtles are easier to feed in captivity because most of them will eat either plants or canned dog food. However, aquatic turtles must be fed in the water, since they cannot eat on land.

Some lizards, especially skinks and geckos, make very good pets because they continue to eat well in captivity. But they must be kept well supplied with insects.

Reptiles should be kept either in glass aquariums with wire-mesh tops where they will be protected from drafts, or in specially built cages. The cages must be escape proof. While turtles are easy to contain, snakes and lizards can escape through extremely small holes and can be very difficult to recapture.

Coarse sand, plants, branches, rocks, and a pan of water placed inside its cage will duplicate a reptile's natural environment. A caged reptile should never be left in the sun. It can easily become overheated and die.

Reptiles are fascinating to watch. However, in most cases it is best to keep captured reptiles only a few days. Study them and then return them to the very same spot where you found them. If you should decide to keep a reptile for a pet, learn as much as possible about it *before* you get it. Your library, local nature center, and zoo can offer you good advice on captive reptile care.

box turtle

INDEX